The Gingerbread Man

by Timothy S. Donehoo
Illustrated by Marcelo Elizalde

Meredith® Books
Des Moines, Iowa

Guide for Parents

As your child's first teacher, you are instrumental in helping him or her become a reader. My Turn, Your Turn readers are designed to support you in guiding your emerging reader. Your child can learn skills necessary to read by reading aloud with you!

The skills needed for reading include word recognition, text comprehension, vocabulary, and fluency. Fluency is the ability to read with accuracy, speed, and expression. Rather than reading word by word, fluent readers group words into meaningful chunks. They pause at the right time and read aloud with expression. The more fluent the reader, the better she or he comprehends.

My Turn, Your Turn readers use child-adult repeated oral reading practice to increase these important skills. "Parent pages" on the left-hand side move the plot along. "Child pages" on the right-hand side contain repetitive, rhyming, easy-to-remember sentences, so your child meets with reading success. And early success with books helps your child become a good reader. Through repeated read-alouds, your child reads predictable, patterned text aloud several times per book, which will help to increase reading fluency.

Your positive feedback guides your child's performance. Children who reread passages orally as they receive feedback and praise become better readers.

My Turn, Your Turn readers provide:
- Familiar tales that will engage your child.
- Clear, appealing illustrations that provide clues about the story.
- Simple designs that help familiarize your child with print.
- Predictable sentences that are repetitive, patterned, and often rhyming. Before long, your child will recognize familiar words.
- The opportunity to spend quality time together.

Before reading a My Turn, Your Turn book for the first time:
- **GET COZY.** Find a comfortable, quiet spot to read together.
- **SHOW THE COVER.** Have your child talk about the picture. Read your child the title and author's name.
- **TAKE A "BOOK WALK."** As you flip through the pages, look at the pictures and talk about them. (You might say, "Let's see who the character on the cover meets. Where does it look like he is going?")

Reading the book:

- **MODEL FLUENT READING.** For a first reading, read through the entire book aloud. Read naturally and expressively, as if you were speaking. This helps your child learn how a fluent reader sounds.
- **MATCH PRINT TO SPOKEN WORDS.** Place your finger below each word to help your child follow along.
- **ASK QUESTIONS.** Challenge your child to predict what will happen next.
- **ENGAGE YOUR CHILD IN REPEATED ORAL READING WITH GUIDANCE.** After one or more readings, invite your child to take a turn. Model how to read your child's page, then read it together. Ask your child to reread it the way you did. Provide help and encouragement.

When it's your child's turn to read:

- **HAM IT UP!** Suggest that your child use different voices for different characters' dialogue.
- **SET UP SUCCESS.** The last lines on the parent page are set in italics. When you come to these lines, use them to prompt your child to read his or her part by saying the first few words in a manner that lets your child know it is time to take over.
- **OFFER HELP.** If your child gets stuck on a word, you might say, "Could this word be 'fast'?" or "Look at the picture. What word makes sense?" If he or she is still stuck, provide the word, so comprehension is not interrupted.
- **PRAISE YOUR CHILD.** Compliment fluent reading and effort. Before you know it, your child may want to read the entire book independently!

After reading:

- **TALK ABOUT THE BOOK.** Have your child select a favorite part. Encourage a retelling of the story as your child looks at the pictures.
- **READ THE BOOK OVER AND OVER.** The more your child rereads, the more his or her accuracy, expression, and confidence will increase.
- **CREATE A BOND.** Use My Turn, Your Turn readers for your child to share with a grandparent. Or suggest a read-aloud where your child and an older sibling alternate pages while the rest of the family listens.
- **BE A READING ROLE MODEL.** Seeing you read will have a positive effect on your child's attitude toward reading.*
- **READ TOGETHER DAILY.** Try to read at least 20 minutes a day. There is a direct relationship between reading skills and time spent reading.**
- **MOST OF ALL, HAVE FUN READING!** The more fun you both have reading, the more likely your child is to read!

Footnotes:
*According to the National Institute for Literacy
**According to the National Assessment of Educational Progress

Once upon a time, Mrs. O'Grady wanted to bake a
sweet, little Gingerbread Man. She mixed the batter,
rolled out the dough, and dressed him up. When she
was done, she put him in the oven. But a few minute
later, Mrs. O'Grady heard a tiny voice crying, "Let me
out! Let me out!" So she opened the oven door.

The little Gingerbread Man popped out of the oven
and ran. Mrs. O'Grady said, "Stop, little Gingerbread
Man. I want to eat you up!" But he was too fast. The
little Gingerbread Man ran away singing . . .

"Run, run as fast as you can.
You can't eat me.
I'm the Gingerbread Man."

"Run, run as fast as you can.
You can't eat me.
I'm the Gingerbread Man."

Soon, the little Gingerbread Man ran up to a waddling duck. When the duck saw the little Gingerbread Man, he quacked,

"Quack! Quack!
Stop, little Gingerbread Man!
I want to eat you up!"

"Quack! Quack!
Stop, little Gingerbread Man!
I want to eat you up!"

But the little Gingerbread Man was too fast.
He ran away singing . . .

"Run, run as fast as you can.
You can't eat me.
I'm the Gingerbread Man."

"Run, run as fast as you can.
You can't eat me.
I'm the Gingerbread Man."

Soon, the little Gingerbread Man ran up to a
grass-chewing cow. When the cow saw the
Gingerbread Man, she mooed,

"Moo! Moo!
  Stop, little Gingerbread Man!
  I want to eat you up!"

"Moo! Moo!
Stop, little Gingerbread Man!
I want to eat you up!"

But the little Gingerbread Man was too fast.
He ran away singing . . .

"Run, run as fast as you can.
You can't eat me.
I'm the Gingerbread Man."

"Run, run as fast as you can.
You can't eat me.
I'm the Gingerbread Man."

Soon, the little Gingerbread Man ran up to
a trotting horse. When the horse saw the
Gingerbread Man, he neighed,

*"Neigh! Neigh!
Stop, little Gingerbread Man!
I want to eat you up!"*

"Neigh! Neigh!
Stop, little Gingerbread Man!
I want to eat you up!"

But the little Gingerbread Man was too fast.
He ran away singing . . .

"Run, run as fast as you can.
You can't eat me.
I'm the Gingerbread Man."

"Run, run as fast as you can.
You can't eat me.
I'm the Gingerbread Man."

Soon, the little Gingerbread Man ran up to
a hunting fox. When the fox saw the little
Gingerbread Man, she barked,

"Bark! Bark!
Stop, little Gingerbread Man!
I want to talk to you!"

"Bark! Bark!
  Stop, little Gingerbread Man!
  I want to talk to you!"

But the little Gingerbread Man was too fast.
He ran away singing . . .

"Run, run as fast as you can.
You can't eat me.
I'm the Gingerbread Man."

"Run, run as fast as you can.
You can't eat me.
I'm the Gingerbread Man."

But the sly fox said, "Bark, bark! I don't want to eat you. I want to be your friend."

Soon, the little Gingerbread Man came to a river. The fox said, "I'll help you cross the river. Jump onto my tail." So he did. But before long the fox said, "You are too heavy on my tail. Jump on my back." So he did. After a while the fox said, "You are too heavy on my back. Jump on my nose." So he did.

Then, that sly fox quickly tilted back her head and opened her mouth. *SNAP!* And that was the end of the little Gingerbread Man.

The end!

The end!

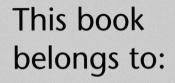

This book belongs to:

_____

_____

My Turn, Your Turn is a trademark of the Meredith Corporation.

ISBN: 0-696-22853-X

We welcome your comments and suggestions. Write to us at:
Meredith Books, Children's Books
1716 Locust St.
Des Moines, IA 50309-3023.
Or visit us at: meredithbooks.com